Dear Parent:

Congratulations! Your child is taking the first steps on an exciting journey. The destination? Independent reading!

STEP INTO READING® will help your child get there. The program offers five steps to reading success. Each step includes fun stories and colorful art. There are also Step into Reading Sticker Books, Step into Reading Math Readers, Step into Reading Write-In Readers, Step into Reading Phonics Readers, and Step into Reading Phonics First Steps! Boxed Sets—a complete literacy program with something for every child.

Learning to Read, Step by Step!

Ready to Read Preschool–Kindergarten
• big type and easy words • rhyme and rhythm • picture clues
For children who know the alphabet and are eager to begin reading.

Reading with Help Preschool–Grade 1
• basic vocabulary • short sentences • simple stories
For children who recognize familiar words and sound out new words with help.

Reading on Your Own Grades 1–3
• engaging characters • easy-to-follow plots • popular topics
For children who are ready to read on their own.

Reading Paragraphs Grades 2–3
• challenging vocabulary • short paragraphs • exciting stories
For newly independent readers who read simple sentences with confidence.

Ready for Chapters Grades 2–4
• chapters • longer paragraphs • full-color art
For children who want to take the plunge into chapter books but still like colorful pictures.

STEP INTO READING® is designed to give every child a successful reading experience. The grade levels are only guides. Children can progress through the steps at their own speed, developing confidence in their reading, no matter what their grade.

Remember, a lifetime love of reading starts with a single step!

For Henya, with love
—A.W.P.

For Heidi, Shana, and Suzy
—J.G.

Text copyright © 2005 by Ann Whitford Paul. Illustrations copyright © 2005 by Jan Gerardi. All rights reserved under International and Pan-American Copyright Conventions. Published in the United States by Random House Children's Books, a division of Random House, Inc., New York, and simultaneously in Canada by Random House of Canada Limited, Toronto.

www.stepintoreading.com

Educators and librarians, for a variety of teaching tools, visit us at
www.randomhouse.com/teachers

Library of Congress Cataloging-in-Publication Data
Paul, Ann Whitford.
Hop! hop! hop! / by Ann Whitford Paul ; illustrated by Jan Gerardi. — 1st ed.
   p.   cm. — (Step into reading. A step 1 book)
SUMMARY: Little Rabbit follows Big Rabbit as he hops over puddles and rocks, until Little Rabbit discovers that things work better if he does it his own way.
ISBN 0-375-82857-5 (trade) — ISBN 0-375-92857-X (lib. bdg.)
[1. Size—Fiction. 2. Individuality—Fiction. 3. Rabbits—Fiction.] I. Gerardi, Jan, ill. II. Title.
III. Series: Step into reading. Step 1.
PZ7.P278338Ho 2005   [E]—dc22   2004008900

Printed in the United States of America   First Edition   10 9 8 7 6 5 4 3 2 1

STEP INTO READING, RANDOM HOUSE, and the Random House colophon are registered trademarks of Random House, Inc.

Hop! Hop! Hop!

by Ann Whitford Paul

illustrated by Jan Gerardi

Random House 🏠 New York

Big Rabbit

hops big hops.

Little Rabbit
hops little hops.

Big Rabbit hops
over the flower.

Little Rabbit hops—

SQUISH!

Big Rabbit hops
over the puddle.

Little Rabbit hops—

SPLASH!

Big Rabbit hops

over the root.

Little Rabbit hops—

PLUNK!

Big Rabbit hops
over the log.

Little Rabbit hops—

CLUNK!

Big Rabbit hops
over the rock.

23

Little Rabbit hops—

SMACK!

Big Rabbit hops
over the stump.

Little Rabbit hops—

No!

Little Rabbit stops.

He looks at the stump.

He looks at Big Rabbit.

Then Little Rabbit hops—

Hop!

Hop!

Hop!—

around the stump.